Eye of the Storm

CHASING STORMS WITH WARREN FAIDLEY

Eye of the Storm

CHASING STORMS WITH WARREN FAIDLEY

STEPHEN KRAMER

PHOTOGRAPHS BY

WARREN FAIDLEY

G. P. PUTNAM'S SONS NEW YORK

For my nephews and nieces:
Jim, John, Amy, Bailey, Noah, and Anne
—SK

To the teachers of children
—WF

Library of Congress Cataloging-in-Publication Data
Kramer, Stephen P.   Eye of the storm: chasing storms with Warren
Faidley/Stephen Kramer; photographs by Warren Faidley.   p.   cm.
Includes bibliographical references.
Summary: Storm chaser Warren Faidley discusses the techniques,
dangers, and difficulties of photographing lightning, tornadoes,
and hurricanes.
1. Storms—Juvenile literature. 2. Storms—Pictorial works—Juvenile
literature. 3. Photography—Scientific applications—Juvenile litera-
ture. 4. Faidley, Warren. [1. Storms. 2. Photography. 3.Faidley,
Warren.] I. Faidley, Warren. ill. II. Title.
QC941.3.A58 1997 778.9'955155—dc20 96-19296 CIP AC
ISBN 0-399-23029-7

10 9 8 7 6 5 4 3

Contents

Storm Chasing

In the evening shadows, a dusty black truck rolls along a dirt road. A rattlesnake feels the vibrations, lifts its head, and crawls off into the rocks. Giant saguaros sprout from the hillsides, arms held high. Somewhere in the distance, a cactus wren calls. But Warren Faidley isn't looking for rattlesnakes, saguaros, or cactus wrens.

He stares through the windshield, eyes glued to a cauliflower-shaped cloud. Behind the cloud, the setting sun turns the sky the color of a ripe peach. Warren has been watching this cloud, and hoping, for almost thirty minutes. The truck heads toward a hill with a clear view of the sky.

Suddenly, a jagged bolt of lightning shoots from the cloud.

"That's it," says Warren.

The truck speeds to the top of the hill and Warren jumps out, arms full of photographic equipment. His fingers fly as he unfolds tripods, mounts his cameras, and points them toward the cloud. Before the road dust has settled, the cameras are clicking.

For twenty minutes, lightning erupts from the cloud. Warren moves back and forth between the cameras—peering through viewfinders, changing film,

switching lenses. Tomorrow, when the film is developed, Warren will know whether he had a successful night. In the meantime, he stands and watches, hoping his cameras are capturing the spectacular lights and colors of the evening thunderstorm.

Watching the Sky

From earliest times, people have watched the sky. Astrologers used the positions of the stars to predict the future. Storytellers used rainbows, winds, the sun and moon to weave tales about the past. Farmers, shepherds, and sailors have all watched the clouds, wondering what tomorrow's weather will be like.

The spectacular storms that sometimes appear in the sky have helped to make weather one of the most mysterious of all natural forces. Myths and legends from around the world describe the fear and awe people felt as they watched lightning explode from a cloud or a tornado appear on the horizon, or listened to the howling winds of a hurricane.

For some people, storms have an irresistible call. These storm chasers head for the mountains, prairies, or seacoasts whenever weather conditions are right.

People chase storms for many reasons. Some storm chasers are scientists, who use video cameras, Doppler radar, and other instruments to learn about what happens in a tornado or a thunderstorm. Photographers follow storms to try to capture the beauty of wind and sky on film. Still other people chase storms in order to catch a brief glimpse of the awesome power of nature.

Warren Faidley: Storm Chaser

Warren Faidley lives in Tucson, Arizona, with a one-toothed cat named Megamouth. He has been interested in storms for almost as long as he can remember.

Warren still remembers the tremendous thunderstorms he saw as a boy in Tucson. Tucked safely in bed, he watched the lightning and listened to the thunder. After the storms had passed, he fell asleep to the smell of wet creosote bushes outside his window.

Warren also had his first encounter with windstorms when he was a boy. Dust devils—spinning columns of wind that look like small tornadoes—often formed in the dusty vacant lots of his neighborhood. One day Warren decided to put on safety goggles and a heavy jacket, and ride his bike into the center of a dust devil. He'll never forget the excitement he felt when he rode through the wall of swirling winds:

"The inside of the devil was still and almost dust free. The light was orange, filtered, I guess, by the wall of dirt that was spinning around me. This rotating wall was filled with all kinds of debris, including tumbleweeds and newspaper pages. Looking up, I could see the very blue sky."

Becoming a Storm Chaser

Warren hadn't always planned to be a storm chaser. He enjoyed studying science in school, and he loved being outside. But he didn't really become interested in taking pictures of the sky until he was working as a photographer for a newspaper.

Warren began by trying to take pictures of lightning from the balcony of his apartment. Although the pictures didn't turn out very well, he soon found himself spending more and more time taking pictures of lightning on summer evenings. Warren read everything he could about weather, and he began to dream about making a living as a weather photographer.

The storm that started Warren's career arrived in Tucson long after the end of the summer thunderstorm season. On that October afternoon, Warren glanced out the back window of his apartment and saw the sharp edges of the storm cloud. He grabbed his equipment, loaded his car, and drove toward a highway underpass on the east side of town.

When Warren reached the underpass, lightning was flashing just a few miles from it. Snatching up his equipment, he scrambled up the steep bank toward a dry ledge where he could set up his cameras. As he set up his tripods, a huge lightning bolt leaped from a

cloud about a mile away, striking the ground next to an air traffic control tower.

But the storm was moving quickly. Suddenly, the air was filled with wind and rain, cutting off the view of any lightning to the east. Warren looked overhead and saw small lightning bolts leaping between the clouds. He knew there was about to be another large bolt—and he was pretty sure that the next big flash would be to the west, on the other side of the underpass.

Warren knew he had to get to the other side of the underpass right away. There wasn't enough room between the ledge and the top of the overpass to walk upright, so he scooted along on his knees. He grabbed hold of overhead rain gutters to keep his balance in the darkness.

Suddenly, Warren stuck his hand into a tangle of thick cobwebs. He quickly pulled his hand back. Then he pointed his penlight toward the ledge and gutters. The whole walkway was lined with webs, and rainwater washing through cracks in the concrete overhead was driving out hundreds of angry black widow spiders!

Ka-boom! A huge bolt of lightning flashed overhead. Warren knew the next bolt would strike somewhere on the west side of the underpass, and he knew he had one chance to capture it. Pushing ahead in the darkness, he used the legs of his tripod as a broom, sweeping aside the cobwebs and trying to brush off any spiders that landed on his clothes.

Near the end of the underpass, and clear of the spider webs, he decided to set up his cameras. The air was sizzling, and Warren could feel that something was about to happen. He slid a few feet down the rough concrete embankment, using his hands and the soles of his shoes as brakes. When the cameras were set up, Warren quickly wiped the raindrops off the lenses. Then he moved back up the slope to a safer place to wait.

Seconds later, he heard a loud crackling, and at the same time he saw a blinding flash of pure, white light. It sounded as if the sky were being torn apart. Next

came the boom of a thunderclap roaring through the underpass. It had the energy of a bomb blast, and it lifted Warren's body right off the ground.

Warren lost his hold on the slope and began sliding downhill toward his cameras. He knew that he had to close the shutters on them without bumping the tripods—or the film with the lightning would blur and be ruined. Using his hands and feet and the seat of his pants as brakes on the concrete, Warren slid to a stop just above his tripods. Carefully, he reached up and closed the shutters on the cameras. Then he looked down at his palms and saw that they were covered with blood.

Warren stayed under the underpass long after the storm had passed, thinking about what had just happened. He knew the lightning strike had been close, because when he closed his eyes he could still see its jagged outline.

The next morning, when Warren had his film developed, he was astonished by what he saw. In the center of one of the rolls was an incredible image of a lightning bolt hitting a light pole in front of some metal storage tanks. The picture had been taken from less than four hundred feet. Warren knew that he was holding the closest good picture ever taken of a lightning bolt hitting an object.

The lightning picture changed Warren's life. It was analyzed and written about by Dr. E. Philip Krider, a lightning scientist at the University of Arizona. *Life* magazine printed the picture, calling Warren a storm chaser. *National Geographic* called, wanting to film a special program about his work. The *National Enquirer* ran an article about Warren, calling him a "fearless spider-fighting photog." He even got a call from a Japanese game show that wanted to feature him on a TV program in which contestants try to guess a mystery guest's occupation. Warren began making enough money from selling his pictures that he could think about being a full-time storm chaser.

What Happens to Warren's Photos After He Takes Them?

You've probably seen some of Warren's photographs. His pictures of lightning, tornadoes, and hurricanes have appeared in books, magazines, newspapers, advertisements, and scientific films. One of his lightning pictures was even used on stage passes for rock concerts by singer Paul McCartney.

Warren's business is called a stock photo agency. It's like a library of sky and storm photographs. People pay him for the use of his photos.

Suppose, for example, that you are a magazine editor. If you need a lightning photo for an article, you could go out and try to take a picture of lightning yourself. But you might have to wait a very long time for the right kind of storm, and unless you have lots of practice your lightning photograph probably won't be very good.

An easier way of getting a good lightning photo is to write to Warren. He'll send you samples, and you can select the one you like. Then, after sending Warren a fee, you can use the photo in your magazine.

When Warren began selling his lightning photos, he found that people were also asking for pictures of tornadoes and hurricanes. He didn't have photographs of these kinds of storms, so he read everything he could find about tornadoes and hurricanes—and he made plans to photograph them as well.

| April | May | June | July | August | September | October |

Storm Seasons and Chasing

Storms are caused by certain kinds of weather patterns. The same patterns are found in the same areas year after year. For example, every spring, large areas of cool, dry air and warm, moist air collide over the central United States. If the winds are right, tornado-producing thunderstorms appear. That's why tornadoes in the south central United States are most likely to happen in spring. During July and August, shifting winds push moisture from the south up into the Arizona desert. When the cool, moist air is heated by the hot desert, storm clouds form. That's why Tucson has summer thunderstorms. In the late summer and early fall, when oceans in the northern Atlantic are warmest, tropical storms form off the west coast of Africa. A few of these turn into the hurricanes that sometimes batter the east and gulf coasts of North America.

Because Warren is a storm chaser, his life also follows these weather patterns. Each spring, Warren goes on the road, traveling through parts of the United States likely to be hit by tornadoes. During the summer, he stays near Tucson so he can photograph the thunderstorms that develop over the desert. In the late summer and fall, he keeps an eye on weather activity in the Atlantic Ocean, ready to fly to the east coast if a hurricane appears.

Chasing Tornadoes

One of Warren's favorite tornado photos is a picture he took near Miami, Texas. Most of the sky is filled by the lower end of a huge storm cloud. A tornado hangs from the cloud, kicking up dust from the empty prairie, while the blue and yellow sky seems to go on forever.

In some ways, this wasn't a difficult picture for Warren to take. He's an experienced photographer. But before he could shoot this picture, he had to be in the right place at the right time—and that's what makes photographing tornadoes such hard work.

On a spring day, dozens of thunderstorms may develop over thousands of square miles in Texas, Oklahoma, and Kansas, but usually only a few will produce tornadoes. Since many tornadoes are on the ground only a few minutes, they will disappear before Warren can photograph them unless he is nearby. Other times, he will follow a promising storm, only to have it head off into an area where there are no roads. Tornadoes may be hidden by falling rain, making it impossible to take a picture of them. Still other storms may produce tornadoes at night, when it's too dark for Warren to take pictures and too dangerous for him to be out chasing because he can't see what's happening.

A successful tornado photographer needs patience, a good understanding of weather, up-to-the-minute forecasts, and lots of experience watching the sky. Even so, days, weeks, or even whole years can go by without a chance to see a tornado.

Every spring, Warren makes a trip to an area called Tornado Alley. This area stretches from northern Texas up into Oklahoma, Kansas, and Missouri. Warren and his tornado chase partner, Tom Willett, spend about six weeks tracking down giant storms and searching for tornadoes.

Getting ready to go tornado chasing takes lots of time and work. Warren checks all his cameras and

buys plenty of film. He makes sure he has up-to-date copies of road maps for all the states he'll be traveling through. He arranges for friends to take care of Megamouth.

Finally, toward the end of April, Warren and Tom stow all their equipment in Shadow Chaser, Warren's black four-wheel-drive vehicle. Warren designed Shadow Chaser to help him find tornadoes and chase them safely. It is packed with electronic equipment, including radios, radio scanners, and a weather center that can take many different kinds of measurements. Shadow Chaser has emergency flashing lights, a long-

range cellular phone, and special cabinets for storing equipment. It even has a front-mounted video camera that can make videotapes through the windshield.

As Warren and Tom drive toward Tornado Alley, their hopes are high. They know that they'll cover thousands of miles before returning to Tucson. They know they'll chase storms that never produce tornadoes and they'll probably hear about nearby tornadoes they can't get to in time. But with hard work, careful study of weather data, and a little luck, sometimes they'll have a day like the one they had on May 5, 1993.

Tornado Chase Diary: May 5, 1993

Warren keeps a diary, in which he writes about his storm chases. Here are some of the things that happened on May 5, 1993, a remarkable day.

Amarillo, Texas—Morning

I awaken in a motel in Tornado Alley. As I walk to the window to peek out the drapes, I remember that last night's weather forecast showed that this might be a good chase day. Tom climbs out of bed and turns on The Weather Channel.

Later in the morning, Tom and I get the Shadow Chaser ready for the day. I test the radios, check under the hood, make sure the tires are inflated and the lights and wipers are working. We clean, pack, and return each piece of equipment to its usual place. During a chase, there isn't time to look around for a roll of film or lens for a camera.

Finally, we check out of the motel and head for a nearby restaurant for breakfast. Then we drive into town to fill the gas tank and get a few supplies.

National Weather Service Office—Early Afternoon

We arrive at the Amarillo office of the National Weather Service. Here I get an update on local weather conditions, as well as a chance to see a satellite picture of the area. I use current weather information to draw a map of where today's thunderstorms are likely to form. The reports are saying that there is a moderate chance of severe weather in our area, and some of the thunderstorms will probably produce tornadoes. Since the storms aren't expected to develop until later in the afternoon, we take some time off and drive to a nearby garage to have the oil changed in Shadow Chaser.

A couple hours later, we're back at the National Weather Service office to make our final chase decisions. It's beginning to look like the area north of town is our best bet. We pull out the highway maps and start looking at possible routes.

As we leave town, I call a friend and fellow chaser who gives weather reports for a local TV station. He confirms that severe storm clouds are building right where we're headed. He also says that a news team from his station is already headed there.

Near Panhandle, Texas—Late Afternoon

The sky is hazy, but in the distance we can see the tops of anvil-shaped storm clouds. We stop the truck to pick up the TV report. My forecaster friend is on. He's pointing to an area on his map about fifty miles north

of our location. "It looks like we're going to have some severe storms in this area!" he says. We get back into the truck and drive north.

Near Gruver, Texas—Early Evening

The overcast skies clear enough to show a giant thunderstorm just ahead. Then our radio scanner locks onto a message from the TV crew's chase unit. "There's a large funnel cloud coming from this storm," says the message. While the crew describes its location, I look at the map. "They're only eight miles from here," I tell Tom. "Let's go and find it!"

As we approach Gruver, we see the red TV van parked on the side of the road. A cameraman is pointing his camera at a huge, gray-white funnel cloud hanging from the base of a dark cloud. As Tom parks the truck, I use the radio to call in a weather report to the National Weather Service station in Amarillo. The funnel cloud pulls back up into the storm.

We head north, following the storm. As we drive, watching the back of the storm, we can see the clouds darkening and beginning to rotate. The white clouds at the top of the storm take on the shape of a giant mushroom. I'm excited, but I'm worried too. I know that anyone in the path of this storm is in terrible danger.

We follow the storm down the highway. Gradually, it turns and heads back toward the road. We pull over and wait for the storm to cross. While we're waiting, a large semi truck pulls up beside us. The driver opens his window and leans out.

"Hey, are you guys tornado chasers? Is that a tornado forming? Is it safe for me to drive under it?"

"We're not sure if it's going to turn into a tornado, but I'd wait here and let it pass," I answer.

We all watch as the swirling mass crosses the highway. A small funnel cloud reaches down from the storm cloud—and then quickly disappears. I reach for the microphone and call Amarillo:

"This is Warren. I'm about eight miles north of Gruver, just west of Highway 207. Tom and I are looking at a large cloud mass that is organizing and rotating."

"Roger, Warren," replies the spotter coordinator. "We're watching the same area on radar. Thanks."

Now we begin to worry about losing the storm. There aren't very many roads in this area, and most of them run north-south or east-west. Since most storms don't continue for long in these directions, following a

storm is a little like playing a huge game of chess. Tom loads his cameras back into the truck while I check the road map.

We make our way along a tangle of unmarked farm roads a few miles from the Oklahoma border. Since the storm is on our west side, and it's moving northeast, we can safely stay quite close to the updraft without getting in the direct path of a tornado.

Near the Oklahoma/Texas Border—Evening

We keep an eye on the swirling clouds as we drive along. Suddenly, from the center of the clouds, a large white funnel appears.

"Look, Tom! Another tornado!" I exclaim. "That thing is less than a mile away!"

I reach for the microphone and call in another report. The funnel cloud begins to stretch. Soon it looks like the trunk of a huge elephant, wiggling over the green fields below. Then it touches down, officially becoming a tornado. When the funnel touches the ground, wispy little vortices appear around the main cloud of wind. As these mini-tornadoes spin, they kick up dust of their own. I grab the microphone and send another message to the spotter coordinator:

"We're about three or four miles south of the Texas/Oklahoma state line," I explain. "And we're

looking at a large, multivortex tornado on the ground."

Just inside the Oklahoma state line, the road turns slightly toward the northwest. The tornado begins to cross the road a little ahead of us. We stop to try and get some pictures, but the light isn't good. It's hard to see the tornado clearly against the background of the cloud. The air is hazy, and another storm to the west is blocking the sunlight.

"We've got a great tornado here," I say to Tom, "but the light is terrible." We load our gear back into the truck and roll down a bumpy dirt road, looking for better light, while the tornado swirls along beside us.

As Tom drives, he keeps glancing at the tornado. Suddenly he yells, "Warren! There's another tornado forming!" I peer through the window and see a debris cloud forming, sucking up soil from a field.

"Wow," Tom says. "Look what it's doing to that fence!" We watch as it rips a section of barbed-wire fence out of the ground and scatters it across the field. The small area of spinning wind, with no visible funnel cloud above, tears across the fields.

"Slow down, Tom," I say. "I can't see the funnel cloud connected to that thing—and we sure don't want to get hit by it." A few seconds later, the debris cloud disappears.

We follow a maze of unmarked dirt roads until we reach a dead end. As we turn around and drive back toward the highway, we watch as the edges of the storm cloud wrap around the tornado, hiding it from sight. Many sightings of "our" tornado, as well as others in the area, are being reported over the radio. I'm happy to hear that so far the tornadoes haven't hit any populated areas.

East of Guymon, Oklahoma—Evening

It's about 7:30 p.m. when we pull back onto the highway. As we head east, we see a long, thin tornado crossing the road a few miles ahead.

"I bet that's our tornado," I tell Tom. "It looks like it's weakening. We've got to shoot it now!" When Tom stops, I jump out the door, set my camera on the hood to steady it, and go through another roll of film. As we watch, the funnel pulls back up into the dark clouds.

West of Hooker, Oklahoma—Evening

Traveling along the highway, we're joined again by the crew from the TV station. Down the road, I see a huge wedge-shaped tornado on the ground.

"Stop!" I yell to Tom. Tom hits the brakes and we stare through the windshield. The tornado looks like

it's about seven or eight miles from us, moving away, although the fading light makes it hard to be sure. As we watch, the funnel slows down, and then it disappears. We continue on and I spot another tornado. This one looks like a long stovepipe.

"This is incredible," I say to Tom. "We've got two large thunderstorms here, and they're dropping tornadoes everywhere!"

The stovepipe tornado swirls into the clouds before we can get close enough for pictures. As we watch it disappear, I realize that it's getting too dark for any more photos. I know the storms are still active, and I'm worried that the fading light could hide any newly forming tornadoes. Chasing any more tornadoes today would be too dangerous.

Near the Oklahoma/Kansas Border—Evening

As the last of the light disappears, we see two more tornadoes in the distance. One is headed north, rolling into Kansas. As we drive back to Amarillo, we listen to news reports on the radio. "With as many tornadoes as we have had on the ground tonight," says a reporter, "it's a miracle that none of them have hit a town. We do have at least one report of a farm being destroyed, with no injuries so far. But beyond that, we have been extremely fortunate."

Amarillo, Texas—Night

It's 11:00 p.m. by the time we finally pull back into the motel parking lot. As Tom and I unload Shadow Chaser, we're still shaking our heads about what we've seen. The tornadoes we saw caused some damage, but there have been no reports of any deaths or injuries. That makes it easier to celebrate our seven-tornado day.

Tornado Photography

Tornadoes are powerful, swirling windstorms. They form in the air currents of giant storm clouds. As these windstorms descend from clouds, they are called funnel clouds. When a funnel cloud touches the ground, it is called a tornado. The winds of a large tornado may spin as fast as three hundred miles per hour. Tornadoes can destroy houses, uproot trees, and toss around railroad cars.

When Warren photographs a tornado, he is taking pictures of a swirling cloud of winds. Tornadoes are usually dark near the ground because they stir up so much dust. How light or dark a tornado looks also depends on the amount of light in the sky and whether the sun is shining on the tornado from the front or the back.

Warren uses a still camera, a video camera, and a motion picture camera for his tornado shots. The still camera takes photos that might be used in books, magazines, and posters. The video and motion picture cameras make records of how the tornado moves and how it changes. Videotapes and motion pictures of tornadoes can be used on television and in films, and they are also helpful to scientists who study tornadoes.

Chasing Lightning

Warren usually returns home from chasing tornadoes about the middle of June. He has a few weeks to rest and get caught up on his business.

"Chasing tornadoes is grueling," he says. "It takes a lot out of you physically and mentally, and it takes a while to unwind when you get home again."

But the rest doesn't last long. By mid-July, winds begin carrying moisture from the south into the Arizona desert. The moisture, along with the desert heat, produces spectacular summer thunderstorms. And when lightning flashes, Warren is usually out with his cameras.

"Weather forecasts for lightning aren't as critical as they are for tornadoes," says Warren. "With lightning, I look at the information on television or my computer. Within a few minutes I can say, 'Looks like we're going to have lightning tonight,' or, 'No, nothing's going to happen tonight.'"

If there's a good chance of lightning, Warren loads up Shadow Chaser about an hour before sunset. Then he leaves for an area where he thinks he'll have a good view of the storms. The lightning shots he's most interested in are the ones that happen just at sunset, when the sun tints the sky and clouds with beautiful colors.

Like chasing tornadoes, photographing lightning can be dangerous. In fact, Warren says that lightning is a storm chaser's greatest natural danger. Unlike tornadoes or hurricanes, lightning will seek out its targets—especially those made of metal. This makes being out in the open with a camera or a metal tripod very dangerous. Warren no longer photographs lightning as close as he once did. He says that if it's raining on his camera he knows he's too close. But even so, he has had some narrow escapes.

Once, while taking pictures of a lightning storm near Marana, Arizona, Warren set up a video camera to take pictures of himself as he photographed

the storm with other cameras. He turned on the video camera and went to work. A few minutes later, as he walked away from one of his cameras, a huge bolt of lightning blasted overhead. The main part of the lightning bolt hit several miles away, but a small splinter bolt hit the ground about ten feet away from the tripod and twenty feet away from where Warren was standing. The picture was captured on Warren's video camera. It was later shown on *National Geographic Explorer* as the narrator explained, "This small bolt could have killed Faidley."

34

Lightning Photography

Lightning is a giant electrical spark. The light you see during a lightning flash is caused by tiny particles, called electrons, blasting so quickly through the air that they make it glow.

When Warren wants to take a picture of lightning, he attaches his camera to a tripod. A tripod is a three-legged stand that holds the camera still. Then he aims the camera at the cloud or the part of the sky he wants to photograph. Next, he opens the shutter, the part of the camera that lets light shine onto the film.

If there is still some sunlight in the sky, Warren may leave the shutter open for one second, ten seconds, thirty seconds, one minute—or any amount of time in between. The less sunlight there is, the longer he needs to leave the shutter open. Part of being a good pho-tographer is knowing how long to leave the shutter open. If it is open too long, the colors in the picture will be too light. If it isn't open long enough, the picture will be too dark.

If lightning strikes in the part of the sky Warren's camera is pointed at while the shutter is open, the lightning bolt will also be on the picture. If lightning doesn't strike while the shutter is open, all he'll have is a picture of a cloud or a sunset!

When Warren takes lightning pictures at night, after the sunlight is gone, he sets the camera on the tripod, aims it at part of the sky, and opens the shutter. He waits until lightning flashes, and then he closes the shutter. Sometimes he might wait for two or three lightning flashes. Since there is no other light in the sky, these pictures will be dark except for the path the lightning bolts followed as they shot through the air.

Chasing Hurricanes

By the first or second week in September, Tucson's summer thunderstorms are ending. There won't be much lightning until the next summer. But that works out well for Warren, because August through November are months when hurricanes sometimes strike the east and gulf coasts of the United States.

Although Tucson is far from the areas where hurricanes hit, Warren begins his hurricane chases from home. He uses his computer to get information on tropical storms or hurricanes moving toward North America.

"I can't go out and look for a hurricane, or watch one develop, like I can with tornadoes and lightning," says Warren. "When a hurricane is forming, I look at satellite pictures, I listen to weather forecasters talk about it, and I pay attention to what scientists and meteorologists think the hurricane is going to do. Hurricane paths are very hard to predict. Often a hurricane will roar right up to the coast and then stop and go away. So I want to be sure that I'm going to have a storm to photograph before I travel all the way to the east coast!"

When weather forecasters predict that a hurricane will strike the eastern United States, Warren flies to a

city near the place the storm is expected to arrive. Flying is faster than driving Shadow Chaser all the way from Tucson. Besides, a vehicle would not be safe during a hurricane. Branches, boards, and other loose materials carried by hurricane winds quickly shatter windows and damage any cars left outside.

"Hurricanes are the only type of storm where I'm shooting destruction in progress. With tornadoes, you're not usually close enough to shoot the destruction—if you are, you're in a very dangerous place! With hurricanes I'm shooting palm trees bending until they're ready to break and floodwaters splashing over the bank. Those kinds of shots really separate hurricane photos from the others. Most of my hurricane photos are wind shots with heavy rain.

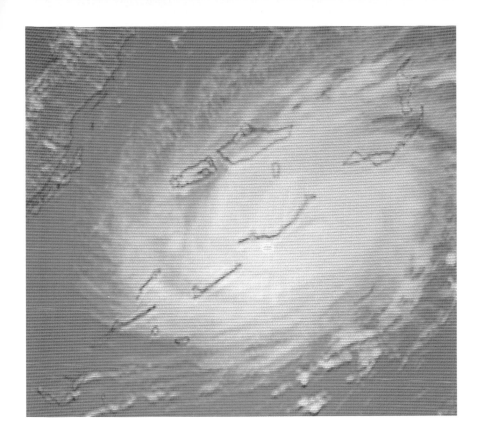

"Finding a place to stay safe while I take hurricane photos is also a challenge. I like to find a solid garage. A good concrete garage is going to be able to withstand the high winds. Another danger with hurricanes is that the powerful winds can lift the seawater and carry it a long ways inland. This is called a storm surge, and it's like a flood from the ocean. When you're picking a spot to stay during the hurricane, you need to have some idea of how high the storm surge might be and how far inland it will go."

Hurricane Andrew

One Saturday, August 22, 1992, after a seven-hour flight from Tucson, Warren arrived in Miami, Florida. He had arranged to meet Mike Laca and Steve Wachholder, two other experienced hurricane chasers. Hurricane Andrew was expected to hit the Florida coast in two days, so Mike, Steve, and Warren had agreed to work together to predict where the storm was going to hit, scout out a safe place to stay, and photograph the storm.

When Warren arrived, the three compared notes. They knew, from weather reports and bulletins from the National Hurricane Center, that Andrew had the potential to become a very dangerous storm. The hurricane was about 520 miles from Miami. It was heading in their direction at about 14 miles per hour. The storm had sustained wind speeds of 110 miles per hour, and they were expected to increase. Warren, Mike, and Steve agreed to get a good night's sleep and meet at noon the next day to go over the latest forecasts. When they had a better idea of where the storm would hit, they could start looking for a safe place to stay.

By the next morning, there were lines of cars heading out of town, on their way to safer places inland.

Store owners were nailing plywood sheets over windows to try to protect them, and people were moving lawn furniture and other things from their yards into their houses.

Mike and Warren found a sturdy, seven-story parking garage in an area called Coconut Grove. It was built with thick concrete walls and looked like a fortress, but the outside walls also had large square openings that could be used for taking pictures. Fort Andrew, as Warren began calling the building, was located on a slight hill, which would help protect it from the storm surge.

Steve, Mike, and Warren set up a "command center" on the fifth floor of the garage. They stockpiled food, water, rope, and waterproof bags as well as their photography equipment. The three took turns monitoring the latest updates on TV and radios.

As the sun set, Warren and his friends waited anxiously. By 11:00 p.m., there was still no sign of the storm. They began to wonder whether the hurricane had changed direction. But reports on the TV and radio kept saying that Andrew was still headed straight for land—and its strongest winds were expected to hit the area where Warren, Steve, and Mike were staying.

About 2:30 a.m., Hurricane Andrew finally

arrived. Warren was watching when bright flashes began appearing in the northeast. The lights looked like fireworks. Actually, they were sparks and explosions as the approaching winds knocked down power lines and transformers. Warren will never forget the sounds of that night:

"At first, there was just the noise of sparking electrical lines and trash cans rolling down the street. But as time passed, the wind just kept getting louder and louder and scarier and scarier."

During the next hour, Steve and Warren tried several times to measure the wind speeds with an instrument called an anemometer. Steve held the instrument out an opening in the wall and Warren used his flashlight to read the dial. When the wind reached 65 miles per hour they gave up.

"I can't hold on anymore," Steve called above the howling winds. "It's too dangerous! I can't hold on!" The winds were carrying raindrops sideways through the air.

"Around 3:45 a.m., we began to hear bursts of breaking glass, as the winds became strong enough to blow in windows. Sometimes the crack of breaking glass was followed by a tinkling sound, like wind chimes, as the wind blew the broken glass along the streets. Inside the garage, car alarm sirens wailed as cars were hit by blasts of wind. Later, even the sound of alarms and the crack of breaking glass disappeared in the roar of the hurricane winds."

As the wind wailed in the darkness, Warren wondered how he was ever going to get any pictures. He worried that by the time it became light, the hurricane winds would die down. He worried about missing the chance to see what was going on outside.

About 5:15 a.m., the hurricane winds reached their peak. The parking garage began to shake. Wind slammed into the concrete walls with the force of bombs. Large sprinkler pipes fastened to the ceilings in the garage began to work their way loose. Several pipes collapsed and fell to the floor.

Now the winds were blowing so hard inside the garage that it was impossible to walk even a few feet in areas that weren't blocked by walls. The roar of the wind turned into a sound like the constant blast of jet engines.

Finally, around 6:00 a.m., with the winds still howling, Warren saw the first faint light of the new day. As the sky gradually turned a strange blue color, Steve, Mike, and Warren looked out on a scene of terrible destruction. Broken boats, and parts of boats, had

been carried by the storm surge from the marina almost to the garage. A tree that had been torn from the ground during the night had smashed into the side of a parked truck. Although most of the buildings around the garage were still standing, many had been heavily damaged.

When there was finally enough light for his camera, Warren headed outside. Leaning into the strong winds, he carefully made his way toward the marina. At times, gusts of wind knocked him to the ground. Wreckage from boats and buildings was still flying through the air. Warren took pictures of the wind bending the trees near the marina and the broken boats on the shore.

Warren continued walking along the beach, shooting more pictures as the sky turned light. After about an hour, the wind began to quiet and the rain became more gentle. Now Warren began to wade carefully toward the marina, taking more pictures of the wreckage ahead of him. Other people were arriving to look at the damage and to see if their boats had survived.

After a tour of the marina, Warren went back to the beach. It was littered with boat parts, clothing, and dead fish. There was even a photo album opened to a wet page. The picture on the page showed a man making a toast from the deck of his boat. More and more

people arrived to see what remained of their homes or boats.

Later in the day, Warren had a chance to see and photograph some of the other activities that followed the storm. A limousine drove up, and President George Bush stepped out to show his support for the people of the area. There were stores with broken windows where everything had been stolen off the shelves by looters, and a damaged bank being guarded by a National Guardsman. Meanwhile, city workers and utility repair people were trying their best to clean up the streets and put electrical wires back into place.

Warren finally returned to his motel, where he slept for ten hours. The next day, when he drove back to the Miami airport, his camera bags were filled with rolls of exposed film. His arm ached where the wind had slammed him into a railing after he left the parking garage. Still, as the airplane took off from Miami, it was hard for Warren to imagine that two nights earlier he had been watching, listening to, and photographing the destructive winds of Hurricane Andrew.

Hurricane Photography

Hurricanes are large, spiral-shaped storms that form over warm parts of the Atlantic or eastern Pacific Oceans. A large hurricane may be over 200 miles wide, and it may travel thousands of miles. The winds in a hurricane average at least 75 miles per hour—and they may reach speeds of more than 150 miles per hour.

Because hurricanes are so large, Warren can't take a picture of an entire hurricane like he can a lightning bolt or tornado. Instead, he concentrates on taking pictures of hurricane winds in action.

Respecting Storms

Chasing storms can be dangerous. Tornadoes, lightning, and hurricanes are unpredictable forces of nature that can kill suddenly. Warren and other experienced chasers understand storms well enough to know what the risks are—and how to stay safe.

"Storms are dangerous," says Warren. "They're nasty. They can do all kinds of horrible things to people. You have to respect them, and it takes years to learn about all the things they can do.

"Every time I go to a storm I tell myself, 'This is a dangerous storm.' Even little tiny storms in the plains, even a little lightning storm in Tucson—I approach all of them the same way. I tell myself I need to be very careful. That's always on my mind."

When Warren chases storms, he helps protect people who might be in a storm's path. He does this by volunteering as a Skywarn spotter. Warren has gone through training to recognize and describe dangerous storms, and when he is out chasing, he radios in reports so that people in danger can be warned.

During the past few years, some storm chasers have become worried about the number of people who think of storm watching as simply a fun activity—like going fishing or taking a Sunday afternoon drive.

There are stories of families driving out to the country and picnicking by the side of the road while they watch a tornado spin across the prairie. One weekend near Oklahoma City, the sides of the roads were so crowded with people who came out to watch a storm that there was no place for police cars and fire trucks to park. Another time, a man in Kansas who saw a radar display of a tornado on TV took off to find the tornado with his wife and young son. He was stopped by high winds that tipped over his car.

People also put themselves in danger when they try to capture pictures of storms on their video cameras. Several years ago, a man in Texas began videotaping a tornado that was moving toward his house. He continued to tape the tornado as it ripped his neighbor's house apart. Next, a bolt of lightning struck, nearly electrocuting him. Still, the man continued to use his video camera to tape the tornado until he was hit by debris carried by the wind.

Storm chasing is only for people who have studied weather, who understand how to stay safe, and who have a good reason for being out near storms. If you are curious about what happens in stormy skies, there are plenty of safe ways to learn more. Start with a visit to your library. Be sure to follow rules that keep you safe—and away from the dangers of storms.

Storm Safety

Tornado Safety: If you live in an area where tornadoes occur, listen carefully to weather reports on the radio and television during tornado season. If a tornado arrives in your area, go immediately to a tornado shelter. (A tornado shelter is a place in your basement or an inside room in your house where you will be protected from winds.) If you are outside, find a low spot where you can lie down and cover your head with your hands. Do not leave your house or stand by a window to watch a tornado. Tornadoes are deadly, and their winds can send rocks, sticks, and broken glass flying through the air like bullets.

Lightning Safety: Do not stay outside to try and watch lightning. Take shelter indoors. If there are no buildings nearby, you can also be safe in a car with all the windows rolled up. Do not stand under trees, power lines, radio towers, or other tall objects, since lightning often strikes these kinds of places. If you cannot get into a building or a car, be sure you aren't the tallest object in the area. Crouch down in a low place like a roadside ditch or a valley between two hills. Stay away from metal objects such as mailboxes, bicycles, fences, and farm equipment.

Hurricane Safety: The best way to stay safe from hurricane winds is to move inland, away from the sea, before the hurricane arrives. After a hurricane comes ashore, its winds begin to slow down. Also, moving inland will help protect you from the flooding of the storm surge. If you cannot get away from the sea before the hurricane hits, be sure to stay in a sturdy building, as high as possible above the ocean. Do not go outdoors during the hurricane. Stay in the center of the house, away from windows.

Tomorrow's Storm

"The sky is like a canvas, and I use the camera to capture whatever's out there. I never know what that's going to be, and that's what makes my trips so fascinating. I may go out, and there may be nothing—which happens a lot. But then again, I know that every day there's a chance I may go out and see the wildest storm of all time."

The sun sank behind the hills over two hours ago. Stars peek out between clouds as Shadow Chaser winds its way off a hilltop and down through a narrow canyon. Warren steps on the brake to give a jackrabbit time to cross the road.

It's a thirty-minute drive back to Tucson, but Warren is feeling good. There were beautiful colors in the clouds at sunset, and the storm he photographed after dark produced some gigantic lightning bolts. Warren is sure he'll be happy with some of tonight's pictures.

Tomorrow, there will be photos to sort, letters to answer, and phone calls to return. As Warren drives home, he thinks of other things he needs to do: buy more film, pick up cat food for Megamouth, take Shadow Chaser in for an oil change.

But by early afternoon, Warren will be listening to the weather forecast. By dinnertime, he'll be watching the sky. And if there are thunderstorms in the area, Warren will head out again in Shadow Chaser, looking for a spot to set up his cameras.

You never know when you'll get the chance to see the wildest storm of all time.

Things You Can Do

One of the best ways to learn about weather is to visit your library. Most libraries have shelves full of weather books with information, photographs, and experiments you can do. Learning the names of different kinds of clouds is a good way to start. Soon you'll find that you automatically look at the sky every time you go outside. Weather books can also show you how to make simple weather instruments of your own.

There are many different careers for people who enjoy learning about weather. Some people become weather scientists, or meteorologists. They often teach and do research at colleges and universities. Meteorologists also work at places like the National Hurricane Center and the National Severe Storms Lab, forecasting dangerous weather. Or they may work in cities across the country, helping figure out what the weather is going to be like tomorrow. People also work as weatherpersons on TV stations, where they appear on the news with weather reports.

People who enjoy learning about weather can also volunteer. In areas where tornadoes occur, some people become Skywarn spotters. By reporting dangerous storms in their area, they can help save people's lives. Volunteers also collect weather data for the Weather

Service. In homes and classrooms, they keep track of measurements such as daily temperatures and amounts of rainfall. These measurements help local meteorologists understand the weather in their area so they can make more accurate forecasts.

Glossary

astrologer: a person who tries to predict the future by studying the positions of the sun, moon, and stars.

creosote: an evergreen shrub that grows in desert areas of the southwestern United States.

Doppler radar: a kind of radar that allows scientists to "see" inside storms and tell how fast and in which direction winds are blowing.

dust devil: a spinning column of warm wind often seen on hot days in desert areas.

funnel cloud: the rapidly swirling winds that sometimes reach downward from a storm cloud. If a funnel cloud reaches all the way to the ground, it is called a tornado.

hurricane: a very large storm with high winds and heavy rain that forms over the Atlantic or eastern Pacific Oceans.

lightning: an electrical spark caused by tiny parts of atoms, called electrons, shooting through the sky.

marina: a small harbor where boats can dock, refuel, and get supplies.

meteorologist: a scientist who studies the earth's atmosphere and weather.

National Hurricane Center: an office of the National Weather Service located in Miami, Florida, that tracks and forecasts hurricanes.

National Weather Service: the U.S. government agency in charge of studying and predicting weather.

Skywarn: a group of volunteers who relay reports of dangerous weather to the National Weather Service. Skywarn spotters have been trained to recognize and describe tornadoes and weather conditions that can cause tornadoes.

spotter coordinator: the person in an area who monitors the reports of Skywarn spotters and passes along the messages to weather scientists, police departments, and others who provide help in emergencies.

stock photo agency: a business that collects and cares for photographs. For a fee, the photos may be used in books, magazines, advertisements, etc.

storm surge: the high waters carried ashore by hurricane winds.

tornado: a swirling windstorm that begins in a storm cloud. The winds of a powerful tornado can reach speeds of three hundred miles per hour.

Tornado Alley: an area in the central part of the United States where tornadoes are likely to happen every year.

tornado shelter: a safe place to stay during a tornado. Tornado shelters may include underground rooms, protected areas in basements, or specially constructed areas in sturdy buildings.

tripod: a three-legged stand that can be used to hold a camera.

tropical storm: a rotating storm that forms over tropical oceans. Some tropical storms turn into hurricanes.

vortex (plural—vortices): a column of swirling wind or water—such as the twisting winds of a tornado.

Further Reading

Armbruster, Ann, and Elizabeth A. Taylor. Tornadoes. New York: Franklin Watts, 1989.

Day, John A., and Vincent Schaefer. Peterson First Guides, Clouds and Weather. Boston, MA: Houghton Mifflin, 1991.

Kramer, Stephen. Lightning. Minneapolis, MN: Carolrhoda Books, 1992.

Kramer, Stephen. Tornado. Minneapolis, MN: Carolrhoda Books, 1992.

Lampton, Christopher. Tornado. Brookfield, CT: Millbrook Press, 1991.

Simon, Seymour. Storms. New York: William Morrow & Co. Inc., 1989.

Simon, Seymour. Weather. New York: William Morrow & Co. Inc., 1993.

Twist, Clint. Hurricanes and Storms. New York: Simon & Schuster Children's Books, 1992.

778.9   Kramer, Stephen P.
KRA
          Eye of the storm.

$18.99

DATE